Susann Opel-Götz

NOW WE ARE COOL

Translated by Annette Hinrichs-Pymm

To Lea and Philipp

"From now on," Leo announced to his little brother, Mug, "we are going to be totally different."

"Different *how*?" asked Mug, nervously.

"Now, we are going to be COOL!" shouted Leo.

"What do you mean?" asked Mug.

"Now that we're COOL," explained Leo, "we will look different."

"Different *how*?" asked Mug.

"COOL people wear sunglasses all day. Even when it rains! Even in the *bathroom*!"

"Why?" asked Mug.

"Because...," Leo pondered. "Because then they can imagine it's a dark and scary night!"

"Of course," mumbled Mug.

"Isn't that COOL?" exclaimed Leo. "Really COOL people get to stay up really, really late!"

"I want to stay up late, too!" answered Mug. "So, what else should we do now that we are COOL, Leo?"

"Now that we are **COOL**," said Leo, "we will watch **COOL** grown-up movies!"

"Movies with monsters and vampires and other stuff?" asked Mug.

"**COOL** people only watch movies that curdle their blood," said Leo in his most terrifyingly **COOL** voice.

"Wh-wh-why would they do that?" stuttered Mug.

"Because…," Leo considered. "Because that's how they get their hair to stick up straight. Sticking-up-straight hair looks COOL, man!"

Mug stared at Leo. "Oh. Okay. But I always thought COOL people used hair gel."

"Hair gel is only for beginners!" snorted Leo.

"What else should we do now that we are COOL?" asked Mug.

cool

1,-

cooler

2,-

supercool

3,95

"Now that we are **COOL**," said Leo, "we will talk like **COOL** people do!"

"How?" asked Mug.

"Simple. A **COOL** person buys a soda like this: 'Hey man, gimme a pitch-black belly blaster—and make it snappy!'"

"What? Why would **COOL** people talk so weird?" wondered Mug.

"Because **COOL** people use code language and—"

"—normal people don't understand code language. They'll think a **COOL** person is an alien—and run away. That way a **COOL** person can help himself to all the soda!" cheered Mug.

"Now you are beginning to understand," said Leo.

"What else should we do now that we are **COOL**?" asked Mug.

"Now that we are COOL," said Leo, "we won't carry old-fashioned school bags anymore."

"How will we carry our books and things to school?" asked Mug.

"COOL people only carry COOL-looking backpacks," Leo declared.

"Why?"

"Because…," Leo thought. "Because that way their moms think every day is a field trip day and won't ask about homework."

"And they get to take extra sandwiches and candy," rejoiced Mug.

"And extra-spicy salami," raved Leo.

"So what else should we do now that we are COOL?"

"We will listen to totally different music, now that we are *COOL*," said Leo.

"What kind of music?" asked Mug, staring at his box of sing-along CDs.

"*COOL* people listen to very loud, angry music all day long, until their ears ring," answered Leo.

"Why would they do that?"

"So they can't hear when their dads yell at them for watching horror movies. Or when their moms ask if they are going on another field trip."

Mug nodded. "I guess that's why **COOL** people always wear knitted hats over their ears—because awful, loud music is way too awful."

"Excellent thinking, Mug."

"So what else should we do now that we are **COOL**, Leo?" asked Mug.

"Now that we are **COOL**," said Leo, "we are going to buy some new pets!"

"But we already have Chico and Peeps!" Mug objected.

"Chico and Peeps are *not* **COOL**," snarled Leo. "A **COOL** person has scary spiders and poisonous rats and blind, three-eyed ninja crickets in his room."

"Why?" Mug's voice began to tremble.

"Well…," thought Leo. "You know Aunt Maggie's slobbery kisses are pretty disgusting, right?"

"You bet!" Mug shuddered.

"Well, imagine buying a big, fat rat in a cage, and calling it Slobber-Maggie."

"Aunt Maggie will be too afraid to come into my room when she finds out that rats and scary spiders live there!" cried Mug.

Leo grinned. "She will *totally* take off."

"So what else should we do now that we are COOL?"

"Now that we are **COOL**," said Leo, "we are going to make very special **COOL** friends."

"What kind of **COOL** friends?" asked Mug.

"**COOL** people have **COOL** friends with names like Phantom, Mack the Knife or Curt the Cobra!"

"Why?" asked Mug. "Mack the Knife sounds pretty dangerous."

Leo kept on talking. "And Laser-Lars and Spider-Max and Lucky-Luke—"

"Can't a **COOL** person also have friends with names like mine?" Mug squeaked.

"Of course! You know, Mug is actually short for **Monster-Under-Ground!**"

Mug the Monster grinned. "And what is your name in **COOL** language?"

"Leo, the **Ever-COOL Overlord**," replied Leo. "*Everybody* knows that."

"So what else should we do now that we are **COOL**, Leo?"

"Now that we are COOL," said Leo, "we are going to misbehave—*a lot*."

"Misbehave how?" asked Mug.

"COOL people burp loudly and toot at the dinner table. They smack and slurp and spill and—"

"—and put their feet on the table when Aunt Maggie comes over for coffee!" shouted Mug.

Leo laughed. "Even a SUPER COOL person couldn't get any nastier than that!"

"But why do COOL people misbehave so badly, Leo?" Mug asked.

Leo scratched his ear. "Well, because...," this time, Leo pondered for a long time. "Because...."

"Because burping is COOL?" Mug suggested helpfully.

"Correct!" Leo crowed. "COOL with a Capital C!"

"Hey, Leo?" Mug stuck his finger in his nose. "Being **COOL** sounds like a lot of work."

"Well," Leo thought. "Maybe a little bit."

"If we misbehave at the dinner table, we won't get dessert, you know," Mug sighed.

"There's a kid at school we call Ralph-the-Rat. He's a bully and a jerk. I wouldn't want *him* as a friend," muttered Leo.

"And with scary spiders in my room, I wouldn't be able to fall asleep," whispered Mug.

"Yeah. And wearing a knitted hat all day would make my head itch," moaned Leo.

"And I really like to watch cartoons. Even if they don't make my hair stick up straight."

"I just got a new school bag with dolphins on it."

"And drinking too much soda makes me sick."

"Plus, it would be pretty hard to build my pirate ship wearing sunglasses."

"Hey, Leo?" asked Mug. "Why don't we hold off on being COOL until tomorrow and go out to play now?"

"Sure! We could dig a tunnel, or go on a treasure hunt, or build a tree house!"

"Tree houses are COOL!" cheered Mug.

Leo jumped to his feet. "I'll ask Dad for a hammer and some nails!"

Mug looked up at his big brother and chuckled. "Okay, man! Gimme a hammer and some nails, too—and make it snappy!"

Susann Opel-Götz was born in Bayreuth in 1963, studied art and literature in Frankfurt am Main and Munich, and continued her studies with book illustration at the Academy of Fine Arts in Munich. Today, Susann is a sought-after illustrator of children's books. *Now We are Cool* is the first picture book that she has both written and illustrated. Susann's art can be seen in many German picture books, some of which have been translated into English, including *A Very Long Nose* by Lukas Hartmann.

We composed this book in Frutiger (14/18) and Fawn Script (16/19) because these typefaces are modern, proportional and *COOL*!

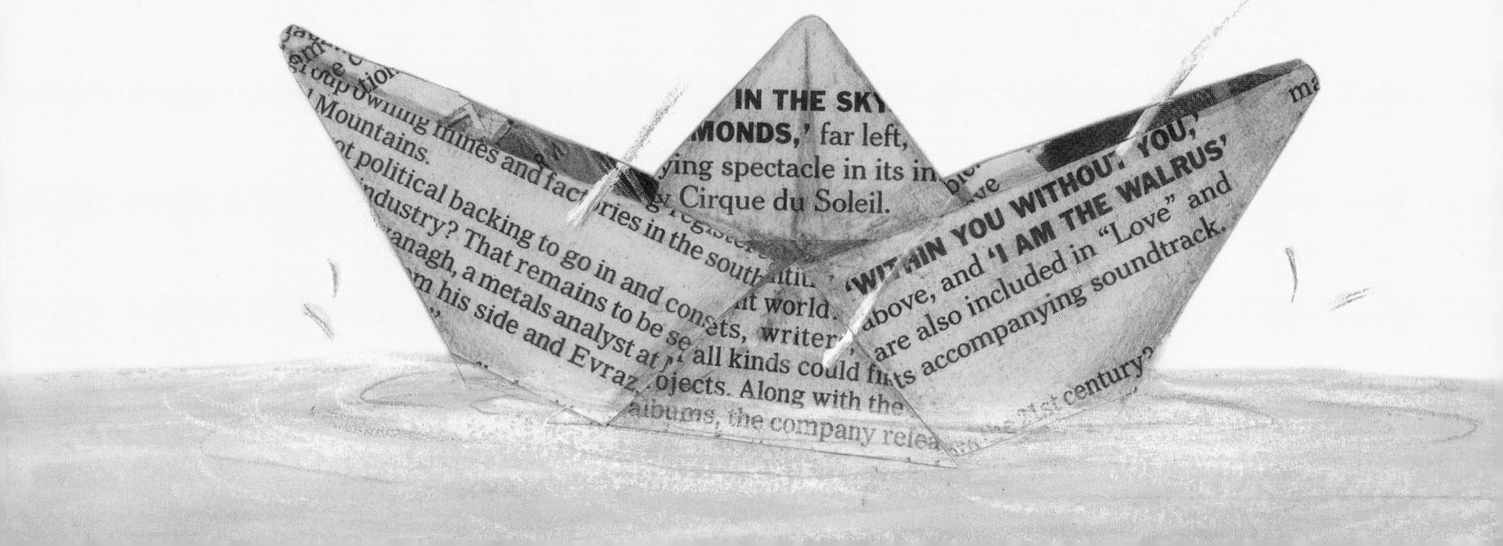
IN THE SKY
MONDS,' far left,
ying spectacle in its in
Cirque du Soleil.
Mountains.
mines and factories in the south
ot political backing to go in and con
ndustry? That remains to be se
anagh, a metals analyst at
m his side and Evraz
ojects. Along with the
albums, the company relea
'WITHIN YOU WITHOU
above, and 'I AM THE WALRUS'
are also included in "Love" and
its accompanying soundtrack.

Originally published as «Ab heute sind wir cool» © Verlag Friedrich Oetinger GmbH, Hamburg 2007
Published in Canada by Fitzhenry & Whiteside, 195 Allstate Parkway, Markham, Ontario L3R 4T8
Published in the United States by Fitzhenry & Whiteside, 311 Washington Street, Brighton, Massachusetts 02135

www.fitzhenry.ca   godwit@fitzhenry.ca

10 9 8 7 6 5 4 3 2 1

Library and Archives Canada Cataloguing in Publication
Opel-Götz, Susann
Now we are cool / Susann Opel-Götz.
Translation of: Ab heute sind wir cool.
ISBN 978-1-55455-235-1
I. Title.
PZ7.O6125No 2012   j833'.92   C2012-901594-6

Publisher Cataloging-in-Publication Data (U.S)
Opel-Götz, Susann.
Now we are cool / Susann Opel-Götz.
[28] p. : col. ill.. ; cm.
Summary: Two brothers decide to change their lives by becoming cool, but soon realise being cool is something other
than how they want to be.
ISBN: 978-1-5455-235-1
1. Conduct of life – Fiction – Juvenile literature. 2. Brothers – Fiction – Juvenile literature. I. Title.
[Fic] dc23   PZ7.O645 2012

Fitzhenry & Whiteside acknowledges with thanks the Canada Council for the Arts, and the Ontario Arts Council for
their support of our publishing program. We acknowledge the financial support of the Government of Canada through
the Canada Book Fund (CBF) for our publishing activities.

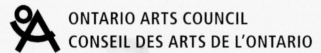

Text design by Daniel Choi
Cover image by Susann Opel-Götz
Translated by Annette Hinrichs-Pymm
Printed in Canada by Friesens